W9-BKN-477

I'm Not Tired Yet!

WRITTEN AND ILLUSTRATED BY

Marianne Richmond

sourcebooks
jabberwocky

Ralphie brushed his teeth
    and had three stories read.
But Ralphie Mix, at age of six,
    didn't want to go to bed.

"I'm **not tired yet**," said Ralphie,
"and, Mom, I see a bug
crawling across the carpet
and underneath my rug."

"I don't think so, Ralphie,"
said a wary Mrs. Mix.
"Could it be that what you need
is a fishy goldfish kiss?"

"I think I do," said Ralphie.

They put their heads together and pulled their cheeks in tight and kissed each other like two fishes looking for a bite.

"**That's better**," said Ralphie.

"Good night, Ralphie," said Mom.

Just as Ralphie's mom
    got up to leave his side,
she looked at little Ralphie,
    whose eyes were growing wide.

"**I'm not tired yet**," said Ralphie,
    "and now a monster's trying to hide
behind the closet shelves…
    Oh gosh, he's there inside!"

"No monster, Ralphie," said his mom,
    "and no bug below your rug.
    Could it be that what you need
    is one big gorilla hug?"

"I think I do," said Ralphie.

They wrapped their arms
     around each other nice and tight
and said "*ooh, ooh*" like mammoth apes
     using all their might.

ooh ooh...

"**That's better**," said Ralphie.
     "Good night, Ralphie," said Mom.

"Goodness," sighed Ralphie's mom,
about to close the door,
when Ralphie Mix, full of tricks,
stayed right there on the floor.

"What now, Ralphie?"
said a flustered Mrs. Mix.
"Little boys must get their sleep,
especially at age six!"

"I'm not tired yet," said Ralphie,
   "and, Mom, there's a problem here...
A big mosquito in my room
   is buzzing in my ear!"

"Ralphie," said his mom, amused,
   and joined him in a huddle,
"Could it be that what you need
   is a cozy polar bear cuddle?"

"I think I do," said Ralphie.

They hugged like cuddly bears before Ralphie's last good night,
growling growly growls as they held each other tight.

"**That's better**," said Ralphie.
"Good night, Ralphie," said Mom.

Thinking they were done for sure,
    Ralphie's mom began to leave
when Ralphie said, "Oh, Mom...
    can I tell you something, please?

"I'm not tired yet," said Ralphie,
    "and my tummy is a little sick.
Can I have a glass of milk?
    That should do the trick."

"Scared and achy?" said his mom.
    "You're being mighty fickle.
Could it be that what you need
    is a caterpillar tickle?"

"I think I do," said Ralphie.

She tickled Ralphie's tummy and he tickled her right back

until the two could laugh no more from the wormy laugh attack.

"**That's better**,"
said Ralphie.
"Good night, Ralphie,"
said Mom.

Once and for all, Ralphie's mom
     began to tiptoe on her way,
turning in her tracks
     to the voice that sure did say…

"I'm **not tired yet**," said Ralphie,
     "and we should talk before you go.
There's some news from school
     that I think you'd want to know…"

"I lost my boots at recess," said Ralphie,
    "and I got a pink slip on the bus.
The principal said me and her
    have issues to discuss.

"But don't worry about it, Mom,
    it'll be all right.
In fact, I think it's time
    for me to say good night."

No one said a thing just then,
as Ralphie's mom sat still,
holding back her temper
and gathering her will.

"Mom," said Ralphie Mix,
"kidding you is a cinch.
Could it be that what you need
is one rock lobster pinch?"

"I think I do," said Ralphie's mom.

They pinched each other's arms up and down with pincer pokes.

"Ralphie Mix," laughed Ralphie's mom, "I do not like your jokes."

"All right, Ralphie," said his mom,
"it's time for bed right now.
The night is late, and you must wake up
for school somehow."

"But I'm not tired…" started Ralphie,
then soon didn't make a peep.
Ralphie Mix, at age of six,
had finally fallen asleep.

Thanks, Adam, for making
bedtime so much fun
for everyone! —Mom

Marianne Richmond is the bestselling author and illustrator of
numerous beautiful books for parents and children to share. She
creates emotional and thoughtful stories that children of any age will
appreciate now and forever.

Text and illustrations copyright © 2012 Marianne Richmond
Cover and internal design © 2012 by Sourcebooks, Inc.
Cover design by Krista Joy Johnson/Sourcebooks

Sourcebooks and the colophon are registered
trademarks of Sourcebooks, Inc.

All rights reserved. No part of this book may be reproduced in any
form or by any electronic or mechanical means including information
storage and retrieval systems—except in the case of brief quotations
embodied in critical articles or reviews—without permission in writing
from its publisher, Sourcebooks, Inc.

The characters and events portrayed in this book are fictitious or are
used fictitiously. Any similarity to real persons, living or dead, is purely
coincidental and not intended by the author.

Published by Sourcebooks Jabberwocky,
an imprint of Sourcebooks, Inc.
P.O. Box 4410, Naperville, Illinois 60567-4410
(630) 961-3900
Fax: (630) 961-2168
www.jabberwockykids.com

Library of Congress Cataloging-in-Publication
data is on file with the publisher.

Source of Production: Oceanic Graphic Printing, Kowloon,
Hong Kong, China
Date of Production: December 2011
Run Number: 16589

Printed and bound in China.
OGP 10 9 8 7 6 5 4 3 2 1

Also available from author & illustrator
Marianne Richmond:

If I Could Keep You Little
I Believe in You
The Gift of an Angel
The Gift of a Memory
Hooray for You!
The Gifts of Being Grand
I Love You So…
Happy Birthday to You!
I Love You So Much…
You Are My Wish Come True
Big Sister
Big Brother
The Night Night Book
Beautiful Blue Eyes
Beautiful Brown Eyes
Big Boys Go Potty
Big Girls Go Potty

Beginner Boards for the youngest child
*simply said…*and *smartly said…*
mini books for all occasions